How Do Dinosaurs Say Good Night?

ALLOSAURUS

PTERANODON

APATOSAURUS

CORYTHOSAURUS

DIMETRODON

ANKYLOSAURUS

TRACHODON

TYRANNOSAURUS RE

STEGOSAURUS

TRICERATOPS

ALLOSAURUS

PTERANODON

CORYTHOSAURUS

APATOSAURUS

DIMETRODON

ANKYLOSAURUS

TRACHODON

TYRANNOSAURUS REX

STEGOSAURUS

TRICERATOPS

JANE YOLEN

How Do Dinosaurs

Say Good Night?

Illustrated by

MARK TEAGUE

SCHOLASTIC INC.

New York Toronto London Auckland Sydney
Mexico City New Delhi Hong Kong Buenos Aires

This book was originally published in hardcover by the Blue Sky Press in 2000.

ISBN-13: 978-0-545-09319-4
ISBN 0-545-09319-8

12 11 10 9 8 7 6 5 4 3   10 11 12 13 14/0   TTL

Printed in China

This edition first printing, October 2008

For my own little dinosaurs at bedtime:

Maddison Jane and Alison Isabelle

J. Y.

To Mom and Dad

M. T.

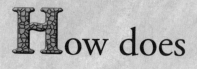How does
a dinosaur say
good night
when Papa
comes in
to turn off
the light?

STEGOSAURUS

Does

a dinosaur

slam

his tail

and pout?

Does he throw
his teddy bear
all about?

Does a
dinosaur
stomp
his feet
on the floor

and shout:
"I want
to hear
one book
more!"?

TRACHODON

DOES

A DINOSAUR

ROAR?

How does a dinosaur say good night
when *Mama* comes in
to turn off the light?

Does he swing his neck

from side to side?

APATOSAURUS

Does he up
and demand
a piggyback ride?

Does he mope,

does he moan,

does he sulk,

does he sigh?

Does he fall on the top
of his covers and cry?

No, dinosaurs don't.
They don't even try.

They give
a big kiss.

They turn out
the light.

DIMETRODON

They tuck in
their tails.
They whisper,
"Good night!"

They give
a big hug,
then give
one kiss
more.

Good night.

Good night, little dinosaur.

ALLOSAURUS

CORYTHOSAURUS

PTERANODON

APATOSAURUS

DIMETRODON

ANKYLOSAURUS

TRACHODON

TYRANNOSAURUS REX

STEGOSAURUS

TRICERATOPS

ALLOSAURUS

CORYTHOSAURUS

PTERANODON

APATOSAURUS

DIMETRODON

ANKYLOSAURUS

TRACHODON

TYRANNOSAURUS REX

STEGOSAURUS

TRICERATOPS